BLOOD MOON

MIDNIGHT
BLOOD MOON

CHRIS KREIE

MINNEAPOLIS

Darby Creek
A division of Lerner Publishing Group, Inc.
241 First Avenue North
Minneapolis, MN 55401 USA

For reading levels and more information, look up this title at www.lernerbooks.com.

Images in this book used with the permission of: © Nattanon Tavonthammarit/ Shutterstock.com (headlights); © iStockphoto.com/kirstypargeter (moon); backgrounds: © iStockphoto.com/AF-studio, © iStockphoto.com/blackred, © iStockphoto.com/ Adam Smigielski.

Main body text set in Janson Text LT Std 12/17.5.
Typeface provided by Adobe Systems.

Library of Congress Cataloging-in-Publication Data

Names: Kreie, Chris, author.
Title: Blood moon / by Chris Kreie.
Description: Minneapolis : Darby Creek, [2017] | Series: Midnight ; 1 | Summary: "A road trip goes south as three best friends drive along the Pacific Coast Highway under a blood moon. Will the mysterious car that is following them lead to deadly danger?"— Provided by publisher.
Identifiers: LCCN 2016025932 (print) | LCCN 2016037653 (ebook) | ISBN 9781512427721 (lb : alk. paper) | ISBN 9781512431025 (pb : alk. paper) | ISBN 9781512427929 (eb pdf)
Subjects: | CYAC: Supernatural—Fiction. | Automobile travel—Fiction.
Classification: LCC PZ7.K8793 Bl 2017 (print) | LCC PZ7.K8793 (ebook) | DDC [Fic]—dc23

LC record available at https://lccn.loc.gov/2016025932

Manufactured in the United States of America
1-41497-23358-8/17/2016

To Tricia,
my constant supporter and cheerleader

CHAPTER 1

Mateo looked over the snack aisle. His eyes surveyed row upon row of chips, cheese puffs, crackers, flavored popcorn, and any other unhealthy thing a person might ever want to stuff down their throat. He had the munchies, and health food wasn't even part of the equation. He was in here for junk, and picking the right junk food at any given point in time was an art form. He factored in his mood, his drink choice, even the temperature and humidity outside. He finally zeroed in on two options: spicy tortilla chips or pork rinds. Decisions, decisions.

Priya and Kristy were on the opposite side of the gas station, grazing through the candy bars. Mateo was always partial to salty over sweet. He grabbed the tortilla chips and walked to the soda case.

On his way, he glanced outside the store at Carl, who was kicking back in the jeep, waiting for the rest of them to finish. It had taken Mateo over a year to rebuild that jeep, and he had done it almost singlehandedly. It was his baby—and his ticket out of Middleton. Mateo was going to be an automotive engineer. That was a done deal. It had been his dream to design cars ever since he was a kid. Now that he was just a little over a year away from college, Mateo was determined to learn as much as he could about cars, get a scholarship to Cal Poly University, and leave his little barrio behind for good.

Tonight was the maiden voyage of the jeep. He'd taken it around the neighborhood a bunch of times, but this was its first time on the open road. He and his best friends were heading up the Pacific Coast Highway. The PCH. The West Coast's most notorious and magnificent road. It hugged the Pacific Ocean and twisted and turned up and down the coast for hundreds of miles. It was the perfect road for the night they'd been waiting for all year: the night of the rare blood moon. Mateo reached into the cooler, picked out his favorite root beer, and met Priya and Kristy at the counter.

"So, what exactly is this blood moon thing, anyway?" Kristy asked Priya.

"It's only the rarest phase of the moon," Priya said as she paid for her snacks. "It's the fourth total lunar eclipse in a row, when Earth completely blocks the moon from the sun. It happens only once every couple of decades."

Mateo added. "And the moon turns red?"

"That's the best part," said Priya. "At the moment of the full eclipse, for just a couple minutes, the moon is bathed in the blood of the interstellar gods and cleansed of all its evil demons. Boo hah hah!" She waved her hands in Kristy's face for scary effect.

"Whatever, Priya," said Kristy. "You know I'm already freaked out. Don't make it worse." Mateo and Priya laughed and finished up at the counter.

Outside, dusk had fallen and a typical Northwest coastal fog was pushing in from the sea. Customers were filling their tanks while traffic sped by along the highway. The air had a slight chill to it, but the heat of the day was hanging on for dear life. Mateo and his friends hoped to time their drive perfectly to be at the Crooked Rock lighthouse when the blood moon happened, just before midnight. Mateo hoped the fog wouldn't ruin their view.

"Come on, guys!" Carl shouted from the shotgun seat. "Time's a wastin'. Let's hit the open road!"

"Let's go!" shouted Kristy. She and Priya screamed and raced to the jeep. Mateo smiled as he ambled along behind them. It was going to be a good night. Definitely a night to remember.

On his left, an old, tan pickup truck was parked at the edge of the lot. It had caught his eye when they pulled in, and seeing it again, he had the same strange feeling that something about it wasn't right. The engine was idling, but there was no one behind the wheel, and he saw no exhaust coming from the tailpipe. The truck was old, but it didn't have a scratch on it. *Why would someone go to the trouble of keeping a run-of-the-mill truck like that in such pristine condition?* he thought. It didn't make sense. It wasn't even close to being a collector's model.

"Hey, Captain Stares-a-Lot!" It was Carl. "Are we heading up the PCH tonight or what?"

Mateo snapped out of his trance. "Sorry!" he shouted. He jogged toward the jeep. His friends were already inside and ready.

"Let's go, night riders!" shouted Kristy.

"Blood moon marauders!" yelled Priya.

Mateo laughed and walked around to the driver's side. When he looked back toward the truck, he froze. The pickup was gone. Vanished. Like it had never been there.

"What is it?" asked Carl. "You look spooked."

Mateo shook the cobwebs from his head. *Get real. Like an entire truck can be there one second and be gone the next. It must have driven off when I wasn't looking,* he thought. Of course that was the explanation. *Trucks don't just up and disappear, you fraidy-cat.* He climbed behind the wheel, started the engine, and pulled the jeep out of the lot.

CHAPTER 2

"She purrs like a kitten!" Carl yelled. They were a half hour out of the city and heading north. The fog had begun to lift. The sapphire blue Pacific was on their left, and with the jeep's soft top pulled off, the cool wind rushed all around them. Music sang from the speakers, Priya and Kristy danced in the back seat as the breeze whipped through their long hair, and Mateo was behind the wheel of his baby, cruising up the PCH, with the first stars just beginning to twinkle in the sky. *This coastline has to be one of the most beautiful places on Earth*, he thought. A group of pelicans floated along the air current, high above the rocks and up the shoreline. *No matter what happens after college, I'm never leaving the ocean. The salt air is in my veins.* He smiled.

Carl was right. The jeep was running like a boss. All the time and all the energy he had put into it had paid off. There was barely an inch of that jeep Mateo hadn't touched. He had done major work on the engine, he had swapped in new seats, the whole front end was a rebuild, and he had even painted the body from end to end. Baja Yellow. With help from his new buddies at the body shop, Mateo had known all along he could make it look good. He had been more concerned about whether he could make the thing run, but so far the jeep was hummin' like a beast. Even better than he had imagined.

"Why do guys always refer to their cars as chicks?" yelled Kristy.

"Yeah, that's so sexist," said Priya.

"You're telling me that if you built a kick-butt machine like this from scratch, you wouldn't give it some dude's name?" asked Carl.

Mateo laughed. "I heard that."

"I don't plan on building a kick-butt machine like this now or at any point in the future, if you must know," said Kristy. "No offense, Mateo."

"None taken." He smiled back at her.

Mateo had made tons of sacrifices to get the jeep where it was. He had taken on two jobs to pay for the car parts, one at a body shop and another at the thirty-minute oil-change place by his school. And he had quit the cross-country team. That one had stung a little. Mateo loved running. He had been competing for pretty much as long as he could remember. After Mateo started winning races in elementary school, his dad told him he had running in his veins. "It's the Tarahumara in you," he would say. "Those are our ancestors. The greatest runners in the world." Mateo didn't always like to be reminded of his Mexican heritage. It's not that he wasn't proud of it—he just wanted to be more than simply another Latino boy, descended from Mexican immigrant farm workers. It was such a cliché.

His parents never missed an opportunity to mention the sacrifices they'd made for him. "We've worked hard to provide you with a better life," they always said. "That's why we came to this country." Mateo loved his folks, and of course they had done a lot for him, but it would be nice to go just one day without hearing about it. Parents were *supposed to* work hard. They were *supposed to* give their children a good life. What did they want? A medal?

When Mateo left the cross-country team, his dad had cried. He had been Mateo's personal coach and running partner ever since Mateo was ten, pushing him to be his best. *Pushed a little too hard sometimes*, thought Mateo. It was like Dad loved watching Mateo win races more than Mateo loved running. When his dad tried to get him to reconsider his decision to quit, Mateo didn't waver. He had made up his mind. If he wanted a scholarship to Cal Poly, he needed to learn about cars, he needed to make money, and he needed to keep up his 4.0 grade point average. Something had to give.

"Is that the blood moon?" Kristy was pointing to the full moon, dangling on the horizon just above the Pacific. It was an incredible shade of pale yellow, with many of the larger craters clearly visible.

"Haven't you listened to anything I've said?" asked Priya. "No. That's the full moon. The blood moon is going to happen at 11:47."

"Could you be more specific?" Mateo asked sarcastically.

"Hey, I know my blood moons," said Priya. "What can I say?"

"What makes it red, anyway?" Carl asked.

"It's actually really cool." Priya sat up. "When Earth gets between the sun and the moon, the moon will start to go black. You'll start seeing less and less of it. When Earth is completely in front of the sun, the moon turns red. It's our atmosphere that gives it that color."

Mateo turned around for a second. "And that's when we're supposed to start howling?"

Carl added, "And dance naked on the beach?"

"No, you dorks." Priya punched Mateo in the shoulder. "But I will tell you something pretty freaky."

"Great," said Kristy. "Here we go."

"Back in 2004," said Priya, "on the night of one of the last blood moons, there was a girl from this area who vanished. A girl from Sleepy Cove. She went out with her friends that night and never came back. None of the friends could explain what happened to her. People suspected they killed her, but no one ever found a body, so the girls were never convicted. Some people think the spirit of the girl is still out there, ready to come back during the next blood moon to enact its revenge."

"Shut up, Priya," said Kristy. "If you keep trying to scare me, I'll make Mateo turn around."

"Who says I'll listen to you?" said Mateo, smiling. "I'd love to meet the spirit of some old, dead chick. I bet she's hot."

"Stop it, all of you," said Kristy.

"Okay," said Carl. "Phone check. Everyone remember to leave your phone at home?"

"Mine's in my bedroom," said Mateo.

"Check," said Priya. "Kitchen."

"You really think keeping our phones at home is going to make the night more dramatic?" asked Kristy.

"I do," said Carl. "Besides, we agreed. Tonight, no distractions: no talking, no texting, no nothing. Tonight's all about the blood moon."

"A night to remember," said Mateo.

Carl and Priya smiled. "A night to remember," they repeated.

"Dumb." Kristy shook her head.

Mateo's thoughts quickly got lost in the painted highway lines and the growing darkness. The others sang along to the latest bubblegum pop song on the radio. He was at peace. Everything felt right. He had his ride, he had his friends, and college couldn't come quickly enough. All of a sudden he felt a lot less like a little kid and a lot more like an adult. He drank in the feeling.

The fog was all but gone by now, and night was definitely upon them. The glow of the full moon over the Pacific was becoming more and more intense. The ocean was calm, with just a few ripples, the ever-so-slight movement making the moon appear to dance magically on the water. Mateo would suggest they pull over soon so he could get out his jacket, and if the temperature kept dropping, he might even consider putting the top back on the jeep. *Nah*, he decided. *Putting the top on can wait.* He wanted to enjoy the thick, salty air for as long as possible.

The road was blissfully empty—in fact, they seemed to be the only ones on it. Just two cars had passed them going south the entire time, which was saying something, considering they'd been driving for nearly an hour. This stretch of the PCH was somewhat isolated— nothing like the summer traffic jam that built up between San Francisco and L.A. thanks to the million tourists that arrived every year. But seeing only a few cars on a beautiful Saturday night like this was still strange. Eerie, really.

Mateo wasn't driving particularly fast. This was a joyride, after all; nothing demanded they make good time. He looked in his mirrors. He was ready to slow down even more to let a speedster pass if one approached from behind—Mateo was all about proper driving etiquette. Slow cars should allow faster cars to pass. But nothing showed up. No speedsters. No vehicles of any kind.

Finally, after a few seconds of staring at the road, he spotted something in his right side mirror. What was it? It couldn't be a car. There were no headlights. He dismissed it and turned his eyes back to the highway.

After a few seconds, he couldn't help looking again, this time in his rearview mirror. And again he saw it. There was something back there. Following them.

Carl saw him looking. "What is it?"

"Nothing," said Mateo. "It's just . . . I can't tell. Is there something behind us?"

Everyone but Mateo turned around.

"It's a truck," said Kristy.

"With its lights off?" asked Mateo.

"Yeah," said Priya.

Mateo checked his mirrors again. "What the heck?"

"It's getting closer," said Carl.

"Maybe it's the spirit of a dead truck driver," said Priya. "Someone else who died back in 2004."

"Shut up, Priya," said Kristy.

"It's getting closer," said Carl.

Even in the darkness, the truck was clearly visible now. It was just a couple car lengths behind them, and it was creeping closer by the second.

"What does he want?" asked Kristy.

"Who knows?" said Mateo. "He's probably drunk. I'll slow down." Mateo took his foot off the gas and waved the driver past.

The pickup truck moved even closer and hung on their bumper as they curved left and then right along the mountain road. "He's a lunatic," said Kristy.

Mateo let the car drift down to forty miles per hour, then thirty-five. Still nothing. The driver didn't budge.

Suddenly, a roar blasted into the night as the truck swerved into the oncoming lane and screamed past them, just inches away from the jeep's side mirror. It was then that Mateo noticed what he should've noticed right away: it was the same old, tan pickup he'd seen at the gas station.

CHAPTER 3

"Where'd it go?" asked Carl.

The truck had disappeared around a bend in the road. When Mateo cruised around the same curve, the truck was gone, like it had never been there. *Just like back at the gas station.*

"Freaky," said Priya.

"Freaky?" said Kristy. "Try moronic and irresponsible. Who drives like that?"

"Did anyone see the driver?" asked Mateo.

"Um," said Carl. "I didn't see one."

"Me either," said Priya.

"Good one, guys," said Kristy. "The truck that just sped past us didn't have a driver. Your feeble attempts to scare me are becoming more and more pathetic."

"I didn't see a driver either," said Mateo.

"Mateo, not you too," said Kristy. "You guys are so dumb."

"It must have been the fog," said Carl. "That's why we couldn't see him."

"Um, but there is no fog," said Mateo. "Not anymore."

"It could be one of those driverless cars," said Priya, smiling. Mateo and Carl laughed.

"Just stop it." Kristy shoved Priya. "All of you."

"Sorry," said Priya. "I'm just playin'. Of course there was a driver. There had to have been a driver. Just because we couldn't see him doesn't mean he wasn't there."

"He was probably dressed in black," said Mateo.

"With no lights on, it was just impossible to see him," said Priya. "Sorry, Kristy. I'll stop. I'm sure you're right. It was a stupid driver making foolish choices. Forgive me?"

"I guess," said Kristy. They hugged.

"Are we still up for this?" Mateo asked.

"Of course," said Kristy. "We're going to the lighthouse to watch the blood moon. That was the plan, and we're not going to let some obnoxious driver stop us."

"Perfect," said Carl. "Driver, you heard the woman. Onward!"

Mateo smiled and stepped a little harder on the gas pedal. He didn't want to say anything more because Kristy was already afraid, but part of him suspected something bizarre was going down. The truck disappearing at the gas station and again on the highway was crazy. But not being able to make out a person behind the wheel? That was the icing on an already freakish cake. Mateo seriously doubted that this was your average truck. *Maybe there's some truth to Priya's crazy tales about the blood moon.*

Mateo quickly tried to rationalize things. *The truck is just a truck, and the driver is some guy in a dark jacket getting his kicks by freaking tourists out. We lost the truck around the corner because the truck was driving so much faster. It made it around the first corner and then quickly around a few more. That's why it looked like it disappeared. What other explanation could there be?* Still, part of him wished that Kristy had asked him to turn the jeep around and take them all back to Middleton. They could go to the Flame, have a few smoothies, some fish tacos. They could be surrounded by people. A lot of people. And they could be far away from the desolate coast and some phantom pickup truck.

"Don't look now," said Carl, who was facing backward, "but our friend is back."

"Are you serious?" asked Mateo.

The girls whipped their heads around. Mateo checked his driver's-side mirror. Sure enough, there it was—the same truck, again with its headlights off.

"What does he want?" shouted Kristy.

"Where did he come from?" asked Priya.

"He must've pulled over, and we just didn't see him in the dark," said Carl.

"I'm not so sure," said Mateo.

"What do you mean?" asked Carl.

The truck accelerated up to the back of the jeep. It seemed to be inches from their bumper.

Priya screamed. "He's a psycho!"

"Let him pass," said Carl.

"Anyone see a driver?" asked Mateo.

The three friends stared at the truck.

"It's too dark," said Priya.

"Of course there's someone in there," said Kristy.

"But can you see him?" asked Mateo.

"No," said Carl.

Mateo again slowed down, and again he waved the driver past. But as soon as he did it, he knew it was a pointless gesture. The truck didn't want to get around them. It wanted to scare them.

"He's passing," said Kristy.

"Really?" asked Mateo.

But instead of flying past, the truck pulled up alongside the jeep. Mateo did his best to look into the cab. He could see some movement inside, but in the darkness it was still impossible to tell who—or what—was behind the wheel.

"What's he doing now?" shrieked Kristy.

"He's just sitting there," said Carl.

Mateo kept the jeep at cruising speed, just around forty. He hoped the truck would get bored and drive off.

The vehicles drove side by side up a hill and around two sharp corners. With the truck to his left and the edge of the road to his right, there was absolutely no room for error. Mateo glanced at the truck, but he had to keep his eyes on the road and the jeep safely on the pavement. They swerved around yet another bend. At any moment an oncoming car, hidden from view, could be on top of them, crashing headlong into the pickup.

"You should pull over," said Carl. "He's going to kill someone."

"Where?" said Mateo. "There's absolutely no shoulder." Calling the PCH a narrow stretch of road was an understatement. The only thing separating Mateo's jeep from a steep embankment to his right was about five feet of grass, bushes, and boulders.

Suddenly the truck eased ahead of them just a bit. Almost simultaneously it moved to the right. It was forcing them off the road.

"Look out!" shouted Priya.

"I see it," said Mateo. He pulled to his right, his tires balancing precariously on the edge of the asphalt.

The pickup didn't stop. It kept moving right.

"I'm going to have to ditch the road!" shouted Mateo. "Otherwise he's going to push me off. Everyone hang on!"

Mateo waited just a second—long enough to clear a couple of boulders up ahead in the grass. They flashed past, centimeters from the tires. Shouting "Here we go," Mateo yanked the wheel hard to the right and applied the brakes, not so hard as to lose control, but hard enough to stop before another thousand-pound boulder appeared out of nowhere in front of them.

It was a hard stop. The jeep dipped and dived several times before crashing to a halt. Dust billowed in all directions.

Mateo was clutching the wheel, his knuckles ivory white. He released his grip and let out a deep breath. "Everyone okay?" He took a look around the jeep.

Carl's hands were still braced against the dashboard. The girls' eyes were huge.

"I think so," said Kristy.

Priya checked. "Yep. Nothing broken here."

Nobody said a word for at least a minute. Mateo thought he could hear the beating of his friends' hearts.

Carl broke the silence. "You realize if that had happened on the other side of the road . . ."

"Don't even say it," said Mateo.

"We'd be fish food right now," said Carl.

"He told you not to say it." Kristy took Carl's ball cap off his head and smacked him with it.

"Ow!" Carl grabbed his hat back.

"That truck wants us dead," said Priya. "I'm sorry, Kristy. I don't mean to scare you, but I think it's true."

"It's okay," said Kristy. "This time I think you're right."

Mateo looked from one of them to the other. "We need a plan," he said. "And we need it now."

CHAPTER 4

"What can we do?" asked Kristy.

"We can't stay parked here," said Mateo. "That's for sure." They were barely off the road, with a rocky slope just a couple feet to their right. In the darkness they could easily get clipped by other vehicles approaching from behind. He checked over his shoulder and pulled back onto the highway.

"What happened to the truck?" asked Priya. "Did anybody see?"

"Not me," said Kristy.

Carl looked back at the girls. "It disappeared," he said. He let his comment hang in the air for a few seconds. "Right after it passed us."

"Stop saying that," said Kristy. "That's impossible."

"I'm only telling you what I saw with my own two eyes," said Carl.

"Here's what we're going to do," said Mateo. He had the jeep back up to fifty-five. "We're going to drive. There's gotta be a gas station or a restaurant or something up ahead. We'll pull in, call the cops, report the truck, and get this taken care of."

"Report what truck?" said Carl. "The disappearing one? The phantom tan pickup truck that's been trying to kill us? Is that what we're going to tell the police?" Kristy punched Carl in the shoulder. "Ouch!" He rubbed his arm. "What was that for?"

"Why'd you make us leave our phones at home?" She hit him a couple more times. "How stupid can you be?"

"Let's try to calm down, everybody." said Mateo. *Good one*, he thought. *Tell them to calm down. Maybe you should try taking your own advice. You're the one whose heart is nearly beating out of your chest.*

"Mateo's right." Priya slid over to Kristy and began to rub her back. "We're going to be fine. We'll pull over up ahead, call someone, and this will all be over."

"Then can we go home?" asked Kristy. She started to weep.

"Of course," said Priya. "Then we can go home."

Mateo looked over his shoulder. He and Priya locked eyes and nodded.

The stereo was off, and the girls were no longer dancing. No one was even talking. *We'll put this night behind us*, Mateo thought. *We'll get home safely, let some time pass, and then make plans to drive back up the coast another day. Sure, there won't be another blood moon, but we'll still enjoy a drive up the PCH—one devoid of whack-job drivers and mysterious pickup trucks.*

He was driving fast. Faster than before. Probably a little faster than he should have been. He was also keeping a keen eye on all his mirrors. If the truck returned, he wanted to know about it right away.

"Watch out!" Carl screamed.

Mateo stomped the brakes and heard the screeching of rubber as he slid around a bend in the road. With his eyes on the mirrors, he had missed a sign warning cars to reduce their speed to forty for the oncoming corner. The jeep shimmied a little bit in each direction, but Mateo quickly righted it. "Sorry, guys."

"You drive and get us where we're going," barked Priya. "And you get us there in one piece. We'll watch for the truck."

"Will do," said Mateo. "Sorry."

His heart was pounding again. He followed Priya's orders, keeping his face forward and his eyes on the road. Mateo maintained the proper speed around the next few corners and kept the jeep solidly between the centerline and the white line to his right.

He approached another sign. Relief came over him. This one read, "Driftwood Point—6 miles."

"Six miles," reported Mateo. He gave a smile to everyone. "There's a store in Driftwood Point. We'll be there in five minutes."

"Thank God," said Priya.

Carl patted Mateo on his arm. "Good job."

"It can't be!" shouted Kristy. "It can't be!"

"What?" shouted Carl.

"The truck!" she screamed. "It's back!"

Mateo checked the rearview mirror. Sure enough, there it was: the tan truck, headlights off, on his bumper once more. *Where on Earth did it come from?* he thought. He did some quick calculations in his head. *What else can I do to shake that truck?* Slowing down wasn't the trick. He had already tried that twice. And letting it pass had clearly been a mistake.

Then he remembered the sign. Driftwood Point was just a little more than five miles away. That was nothing. He could keep the truck at bay for five miles, no problem. This jeep, with its new engine and amped-up exhaust system, could easily outrun that old beater. He would gun it. He would outrun that old piece-of-crap truck and get them to safety. Without giving it another thought, Mateo pushed the gas pedal to the floor.

"What are you doing?" shrieked Carl.

"I'm getting us to Driftwood Point," said Mateo. His foot remained heavy on the accelerator. Sixty miles per hour, then sixty-five. The needle on the RPM gauge pointed steadily to the right as the jeep's motor grew louder. "Am I losing him?"

"Not really," said Priya.

Mateo dipped the jeep over a hill and slid into the left lane as he navigated around the corner. *Can't this road run straight or flat for just a little while?* he thought. The twists and turns that made the highway so spectacular and unique also made their escape perilous.

"Be careful!" shouted Carl.

Mateo tried to get the jeep back into the correct lane as they reached another corner, but he overcompensated and took the jeep a few feet off the road to the right. Pebbles clanged around inside the wheel wells as the jeep kicked up clouds of gravel.

"You're going to get us killed!" shouted Priya. "We're never going to make it to Driftwood Point like this!"

"He's still back there!" shouted Kristy.

Fearful that he might lose all control and take them all plummeting into the Pacific, Mateo slowed down. His plan to outrun the truck had been a poor one, anyway: the truck had barely flinched. It remained on their bumper. He slowed down to fifty-five again.

"Now what?" asked Carl.

Mateo looked ahead. The shoulder looked safe. "I'm pulling over." He gently slowed down and eased the jeep into some grass along the highway. The truck barreled past.

"Watch the truck, everyone," said Carl. "Watch. Don't take your eyes off it."

All four of them locked their eyes on the truck. No doubt about it, the truck went from being on the road just in front of them to nowhere—it vanished before their eyes. The fog had lifted over an hour ago. They were on a straight stretch of highway. There was no mistaking it this time: the truck had disappeared like some Las Vegas magic trick.

CHAPTER 5

The group stood, looking over the Pacific,
their bodies butted up to the guard rail as
water lapped against the rocky shoreline far
below them. After the truck disappeared, they
had turned around and driven a few hundred
yards south to a scenic overlook Mateo had
remembered passing earlier. They were done
driving. The plan was to park the jeep and flag
down the first car they saw. The full moon
was higher in the sky now, still just as bright as
ever. "The eclipse is going to start soon,"
said Priya.

"Not the night we were expecting, huh?"
said Mateo.

"Not really," said Carl.

They watched the road. No signs of any cars in either direction, but thankfully, no sign of the tan pickup truck either.

"I feel like I should tell you something," said Priya. "Something else I know about the blood moon."

"What?" asked Mateo.

"There are people who believe in certain types of spirits. Spirits that only come out on the night of a blood moon." Priya looked at each of them. "People have spotted them dancing under the red light of the moon. Legend has it that during the blood moon they steal the souls of the living to join their circles."

"And you were planning on enlightening us with this information when?" asked Carl.

"I was going to tell you," said Priya, "but then Kristy was getting so scared. And, anyway, I thought it was just a silly ghost story. Nothing more than that. I didn't really believe the legend was true."

"Great," said Kristy. "Just great."

"Is there anything else you haven't told us?" asked Carl.

"Well," said Priya, "the story goes that there are certain mystical places hidden in these hills where the spirits lure new souls. If you're in one of these places and you allow the scarlet light of the blood moon to shine on your face, your body disappears and your soul becomes a blood moon spirit for all eternity."

"Really?" said Mateo. He shook his head and paced back and forth. "Really?"

"I'm sorry," said Priya. "Like I said, I thought it was a silly legend."

Just then a set of headlights appeared from the north, driving toward them.

"Finally," said Carl. He bolted for the highway, toward the entrance to the parking lot, his hands waving wildly in the air.

"It could be the truck!" shouted Priya.

"Can't you see?" he yelled back, still flapping his arms. "Its headlights are on!" Carl ran for the entrance.

Mateo looked at Priya and shrugged his shoulders. *Carl has a point*, he thought. *Not once since we've seen the pickup has it had its lights on. Still, running blindly toward a car we can't really see isn't the brightest move in the world.* He and the girls walked more cautiously toward the road.

Carl had made it to the parking-lot entrance. Mateo could hear him shouting at the oncoming car to stop.

The vehicle was approaching fast. Mateo squinted at the lights. They were far apart, and several feet off the ground. Whatever was coming toward them was big. Bigger than a car. It had a square top . . . and a light-colored paint job . . ..

His mouth dropped. "It's the truck!" he screamed.

Priya saw it too. "Carl!" she yelled. "Come back! It's the truck!"

But it was too late. The truck bore down on Carl, who stopped dead in his tracks as it drove straight at him.

"Watch out!" shrieked Kristy.

Carl crouched in fear, seemingly unable to do anything else. *It's over for him,* thought Mateo in an instant. *The truck is going to run him down and that's going to be it. In a few days we'll be attending his funeral.*

If we're not at our own funerals.

But instead of crashing headlong into Carl and splattering his body across the pavement, the truck passed right through him, as if he wasn't even there. Mateo watched in amazement as Carl remained untouched, unmoved, as the truck skidded to a halt between them and Carl.

Carl stood up. Mateo, Priya, and Kristy could only stare in blind horror at the truck. Carl was a statue too. They were waiting for the truck to make a move.

Then something happened—something Mateo had no way of wrapping his head around. Jet-black smoke oozed from the driver's side window and rose up and away from the pickup. Slowly, more and more of it flowed from the truck. It collected in a cloud and hung in the air for several seconds.

Then, before their eyes, the smoke began to transform. "What is that?" said a panicked Kristy. She gripped Mateo's arm. All he could do was shake his head in disbelief. *I have no freaking idea*, he thought. The smoke was taking a more defined shape, a human-like form.

The beast or spirit or phantom or whatever it was hung in the air above them, maybe fifteen feet up, now draped from head to toe in flowing, black robes and outlined in a strange glow. The face of the thing was shrouded behind a deep hood.

Carl was apparently done waiting. His voice rang out into the night. "Run!" he shouted. "Into the woods!" He darted away from the creature, toward the road. Mateo watched. *Does Carl want us to follow him across the highway? Past that . . . thing?*

"Let's go!" shouted Priya. There were two exits to the overlook, the one Carl had taken and another one behind them. Priya ran away from the spirit, toward the other exit, and Kristy followed her. Mateo wasn't sure running into the hills, away from the road and into the dense forest, was such a good idea. But he was happy to put some distance between himself and that spirit, or whatever it was. He took one last look at the creature and ran after his friends.

CHAPTER 6

Mateo lost track of Kristy and Priya almost immediately. The full moon helped guide his way up the hill, but there were just too many trees shading the moonlight—too many dark patches in the crowded woods to really see where he was going.

Off to his left somewhere, Carl was doing a smart thing and constantly yelling into the night. *Yeah, because the last thing he wants is to be alone in the forest with that thing coming after him!* Mateo felt exactly the same way.

"Over here!" yelled Carl. "Everyone! Over here!" His voice was getting louder. Mateo skirted a stand of giant redwood trees and ran up and over an outcropping of rocks. "Over here!" He had to be almost on top of Carl. He scurried up a steep ridge.

"Hey everyone!" Carl was on the ridge, his back turned to Mateo. "Everyone, up . . .!"

"I'm here," said Mateo.

Carl jumped a couple feet off the ground. "Aaaagh!" He turned toward Mateo, bending over and clutching his chest. "You scared me half to death."

"Sorry."

Suddenly Kristy crashed through a thicket of younger trees.

"Thank God!" said Carl.

She ran over to them, panting. "What the heck was that thing?" she shouted. "What the heck is happening?"

"It was a spirit," said Carl. "You heard Priya. It was one of those spirits she told us about. It was driving the truck, and clearly it wants our souls."

"Wait a minute." Mateo looked behind her. "Where is Priya?"

Kristy scanned the group. "Don't say that. Don't joke around." She looked over her shoulder. "I thought she was with you."

"I'm not joking," said Mateo. "I saw you following her. But I lost you guys the minute we hit the woods."

"Priya!" shouted Carl. "Over here!"

"Priya!" Mateo and Kristy joined in. "Priya!"

Then Mateo heard something. "Stop!" he yelled. "Guys. Quiet."

"What is it?" asked Carl.

"Help!"

They looked at one another. "That was Priya," said Kristy. "Oh my gosh, that thing must have caught her. You guys!"

"Help!" The shouts were definitely coming from Priya. She needed them. She was in trouble.

"Let's go!" yelled Mateo. He took off toward Priya's voice, Kristy and Carl right behind him. "Priya, keep yelling!"

"Priya!" shouted Kristy. "We're coming!"

Mateo led them lumbering blindly through the woods. Unfortunately, this was no wilderness hike on a well-worn trail. It was impossible to run straight in any direction.

They dodged right around some redwoods, left past a large pocket of water. After about six or seven twists and turns they had no clue from which direction Priya's yell for help had come.

"Why are you stopping?" asked Carl.

"I'm lost," said Mateo. "Which way was she?"

"Over there." Kristy pointed left.

"No." Carl pointed straight down a ravine. "It was that way."

"Priya!" shouted Mateo. "Priya! Where are you?" Without another call from her, Mateo was pretty sure they'd be poking around in these woods all night.

"Priya!" shouted Kristy.

"What's that?" In a clearing past some trees, about the length of a football field away, Mateo saw a beam of moonlight shining down, illuminating something in the grass. *Could it be?*

"This way!" shouted Mateo, and they took off toward the clearing.

As they got to the edge of the trees, it was clear. "It's Priya!" said Kristy. "Thank goodness. Priya, we're coming for you!"

"Stop!" shouted Mateo. He put on the brakes. "Kristy, stop!" He flung his arms out to prevent the others from running into the grassy meadow. It was definitely Priya in the clearing, but there was something else there too. It floated in the air directly above her. "Wait," said Mateo. He pointed at what he saw. "What is that?"

Now the others could see what Mateo was seeing. Priya was lying on the ground, back to the tall grass, face toward the sky. She appeared to be asleep or in some kind of a trance. About ten feet above her hovered the other thing Mateo had seen. It was white, and it floated and billowed in the sea breeze.

"It's the spirit from the truck," said Kristy, a little too loud.

"Shh," said Carl.

"I don't think so," whispered Mateo. "It's white." Though it was the same shape and size as the spirit that had emerged from the pickup back at the overlook, he got the feeling it was a different spirit.

Which means there's more than one, he realized. *Great.*

"We need to do something," said Kristy.

The spirit drifted, inching ever closer to Priya's motionless body.

Mateo couldn't just sit back and let this creature do whatever it wanted to his friend. *I have to try something.* He took a couple steps into the clearing. Priya was still a good hundred feet away. He stopped and shouted, "Back off!" Mateo stood as tall and steady as he could, feeling the throbbing of blood in his veins. *Relax and stay strong. Don't show any weakness.* "Back off, you freak!"

The thing turned toward him. Mateo took an inadvertent step backward. The face was visible now, and it was awful, like something he'd seen in horror movies. The face was a white skull, but the outline of the bones shimmered and shifted behind the hood, like the face was made of fog or smoke. Then the skull morphed to reveal sharp, wolf-like fangs, and then it contorted into an abhorrent, screaming face with a misshapen, alien forehead.

The spirit's twisting, glowing eyes locked on Mateo, and a horrible shriek split the air. Mateo dropped to the ground, his open palms slapped around his ears. Kristy and Carl fell to the ground behind him. The creature shrieked once more, and the sound tore right through him, his eyes bulging behind his closed eyelids.

As quickly as the horrific scream had pierced the silent evening, it stopped. Mateo got to his feet. The creature had focused again on Priya. Kristy and Carl stood up and sidled alongside Mateo.

An eerie, haunting moan emanated from the spirit as it edged closer and closer to Priya's body. "What's going to happen to her?" asked Kristy. "Isn't there something we can do?"

Before Mateo or Carl could answer, the white spirit dropped to a mere inch above Priya and became a long, narrow plume of smoke. The smoke coiled into her nose and mouth, like a snake burrowing into a crevice, and then, like a snuffed candle, the white spirit was gone. Gone inside the body of their friend.

They rushed to Priya.

CHAPTER 7

"Priya." Mateo bent over her her unmoving form. "It's okay. We're here now."

"Priya. Wake up." Kristy held Priya's face in her hands. "Open your eyes. Please. Just open them. Come on, Priya. Please."

"She's breathing, but she's out," said Carl. "She's out cold." He paced back and forth.

"That thing's inside her," said Kristy. "You saw it. That thing went inside her! We need to get it out!" She shook Priya a little, her breath coming in panicky sobs.

"I've got her." Mateo reached down to lift Priya's body. "We'll carry her out of here and get her to the hospital. Let's go."

Priya's eyes flashed open. Mateo jerked backwards.

"Priya," said Kristy. "It's me. Your best friend, Kristy. Can you see me? We've got you. Everything's going to be okay."

Priya didn't seem to see anything at all. Carl looked over at Mateo. He shook his head.

"I'll grab her," said Mateo. "Let's go."

Mateo took her shoulders, but then Priya's body lurched up into him. He fell back as her body rose from the ground, slowly at first, then faster, out of his reach. Her arms and legs dangled from her torso as she levitated into the sky. "Grab her!" shouted Carl.

Kristy jumped to her feet and flung both arms around Priya's stomach. Priya's body continued to rise. Kristy held on, but when her own feet began to leave the ground below her, her grip loosened and she let go, crashing to the dirt.

Mateo was already moving. He jumped for her body several times, but she was completely out of reach, ten or fifteen feet up and still rising. Higher and higher, until she was above the trees.

"Priya!" shouted Kristy. She looked at Mateo. "Do something!"

Mateo was frozen. *What can I do?* he thought. Whatever had knocked Priya out was now taking her away, and he felt powerless to stop it. *I can't possibly reach her. Not even the tallest basketball player with the best vertical could jump that high.* He watched Priya float farther and farther away from them.

I've gotta think of something. Priya needs me, and Kristy is counting on me. We can't just leave her to this fate. "Let's go!" he shouted. Mateo took one step after her, then another, the others following as he broke into a run. The spirit was moving Priya fast above the trees, with nothing to hinder it, while they stumbled across and around a plethora of stumps and rocks and other barriers. Before they knew it, her body was gone, whisked away into the darkness.

The three of them stopped, panting and heaving at the base of a hill. "It's no use," said Carl.

Kristy was a mess. "She's gone. My best friend's gone." She dropped to her knees, her face in her hands.

Mateo wrapped his arms around her. He really had no idea what to say. Everything had happened so quickly, like a movie or a dream. *Could this be a dream?* Maybe that was it. Could it be possible that any minute he'd be woken up by his mom's voice calling from the kitchen and find himself lying safely in his bed? He shook his head. No, this was no dream. He knew better. This was real, and this reality was something most people wouldn't conjure up in their worst nightmares.

"We'll find her," he finally said to Kristy, trying to reassure himself as much as her. "We'll find a way to save her. We have to."

"How in the world do you propose we do that? Huh?" Carl railed. "How? Her body was just possessed by some white-robed, smoke-for-a-skull, undead beast! You saw that, right? What chance do we have of taking on that thing, not to mention its brother we left behind at the overlook? Now I'm sure you haven't forgotten about him." He seemed close to freaking out in a full-blown frenzy.

"Where do you think it's taking her?" asked Kristy. She was shivering in Mateo's arms.

"Remember Priya's story?" asked Mateo. "She said there are places in these hills where spirits turn the living into one of them."

"You think her story is true?" asked Kristy.

"I don't think we have any other choice but to assume it is," said Mateo. "We'll keep going in the direction Priya's body went. We'll be smart this time and keep the moon in the same spot over our shoulders, to make sure we don't lose our way. We'll find her. And if Priya's story is true, all we have to do is get to her before the light of the blood moon shines on her face."

"Yeah, that's all," said Carl. "That's it. We'll 'get to her.' That's a well-conceived plan."

"You have a better one?" asked Mateo.

"We go back to the road," he said. "Find somebody to help us."

"Look!" Mateo pointed. Earth's shadow had begun to pass in front of the moon. "The eclipse has begun. There's no time to get help."

Kristy began walking away, into the woods, following the direction set by Priya's floating body.

"You can go back to the car if you want to, Carl," she called over her shoulder. "Mateo and I are going to go save our friend."

Mateo looked at Carl and gave him a shrug. He turned to follow Kristy.

Carl stood by himself for only a second. "Wait for me!" he yelled and ran after them.

CHAPTER 8

Mateo led the three of them through the woods. With the lunar eclipse well underway, the night was getting darker by the minute. The last glimmers of yellow light made a final effort to poke through narrow gaps in the tall redwoods. They had been walking for at least an hour with no luck finding Priya. Mateo looked back at the shrinking moon behind them. He didn't need a watch to know that time was short and that the blood moon would be starting soon. *If we don't find Priya fast, we might never see her again.* The thought was a little too much for him. He shook it from his head.

"Are we still walking in the right direction?" Mateo asked.

"The moon's exactly where it was when we started," said Kristy.

"You know Earth rotates, right?" said Carl. "The moon is constantly changing position in the sky. We might be going in exactly the wrong direction."

"It's our best shot," said Mateo. He led them around a stump.

"Can you be positive for one second?" said Kristy. "Our friend's life depends on it."

"Sorry," said Carl. "Just keepin' it real."

"How about keepin' it to yourself," said Kristy.

"You know, sailors used to navigate using the North Star," said Carl. "Not the moon."

"Well, when you figure out where that is, you let us know," said Mateo.

"I have no idea where the North Star is," said Carl.

Kristy shook her head. "Exactly."

Mateo held back some branches from hitting the others.

"The landscape is changing, wouldn't you say?" asked Carl. "The higher we climb, the fewer trees there are. That could be a sign we're getting close, right?"

"Maybe," said Mateo. He had noticed the same thing. They had been climbing a steep hill for at least ten minutes, and the trees had been thinning out. He crouched to shimmy his way under a bush. When he came up on the other side he was standing face-to-face with a sheer, fifteen-foot cliff. Up to this point, their climb had been constant but gradual. There would be nothing easy or gradual about this new hurdle.

The others crowded in behind him. "Should we go back and find another way?" asked Carl.

"No time," said Mateo. The cliff was steep, but right away he spotted some footholds in the rocks. "We're going up. Got your climbing shoes on?"

"Out of my way." Kristy pushed past them and, like a mountain goat, scrabbled up the rock face.

"Impressive," said Mateo. Kristy spent endless summer days climbing with her family.

She might have been scared of spirits and ghosts and other things that go bump—or shriek—in the night, but she was hardly scared of a little cliff.

"You should see me with my cams and slings," she said. She reached her arm down from the top. "Need a hand?"

Mateo smiled. He found some footholds and reached for her hand.

As he hauled himself over the edge, Kristy looked down to Carl.

"Let's go, slowpoke," she said.

"Keep that hand to yourself," he said. "I don't need any help." Carl took one step up, then another. He was almost to the top when one of his feet slipped, leaving him dangling on the wall.

Kristy and Mateo couldn't help but laugh. Carl was hardly in real danger. The fall wouldn't do too much damage.

"Take her hand, macho man," said Mateo.

Carl looked up at Kristy. She smiled down. "Take it," she said.

He scoffed, got his footing back, then

reached his right arm toward hers. She snatched it and hauled him onto the ridge.

"You need to come out climbing with me sometime," Kristy said to Carl as he brushed off his pants. "I'll have you hangdogging and jamming cracks in no time."

"Sounds pleasant," he said.

"Um, guys," said Mateo. "We found her."

Kristy and Carl ran over.

"There." Mateo pointed down into a meadow a couple hundred feet below them. Pointing was a little ridiculous, though. Priya was impossible to miss.

Kristy gasped, her hands going to her mouth. "Oh, my." She looked at Mateo. "It's her."

"Unreal," said Carl.

A dozen flaming torches surrounded Priya's limp form, now resting in the grass. Above her, eight spirits—some black, some white, and some a grayish color in between— circled in an eerie, rhythmic dance. They moved one way in the air, then another, then did a quick spin of two or three revolutions.

Mateo thought he could hear them singing, a sort of wailing hum that vibrated a bit too high and a bit too low for human ears. And he could smell the torches, a scent that reminded him of the incense Priya burned at her house when she'd invite him over for study sessions. The spirits were oblivious to their arrival, keeping their entire focus on Priya.

The ridge they stood on extended all the way around the grassy meadow in a near-perfect circle, rising above piles of rocky fragments at its base. Nothing broke the smooth, green surface below—no trees and no large rocks—giving it the appearance of a perfectly mowed lawn.

"The moon is shining right on her face," Carl pointed out.

The clock was ticking. Soon that moonlight would turn red. Soon their chance to save Priya would slip through their fingers.

"This isn't good," said Kristy. "It's not good at all. Mateo, I don't think we can save her. She's going to turn into a spirit right before our eyes. There's nothing we can do!"

"Now who's the negative one?" said Carl.

"Shut it," said Kristy.

"Hey, I'm not the one who's giving up," said Carl. "I'm not the one who says there's nothing we can do other than sit back and watch our best friend die."

Kristy lunged at Carl and tackled him, taking both of them to the ground. She effortlessly flipped him onto his back and jammed her knees into his shoulders.

"I'm not giving up!" she growled in his face. "I'm not going to let her die!"

Mateo rushed over. "Kristy, it's okay. Take it easy."

"Get off me, you psycho!" Carl grunted and rolled her off of him. They both lay panting in the rocks.

"Don't ever accuse me of giving up on my friend again," said Kristy. Her voice cracked.

"We all just need to calm down," said Mateo. "We'll figure something out. We have to."

Carl stood up, brushing himself off once again. "You two go ahead with your figuring.

I'm going to go do something." He stomped away from Kristy and Mateo, toward the valley.

"Where do you think you're going?" shouted Kristy.

"To save our friend," said Carl.

"By yourself?" shouted Mateo. "What are you planning on doing?"

"Just watch," he said.

CHAPTER 9

"You're crazy!" Mateo shouted. "You can't just march down there!"

Carl had already scrambled partway down the ridge.

"Carl!" yelled Mateo.

Kristy tapped his arm. "Maybe you should stop shouting," she said. "*They* might hear you."

Mateo looked at her. "We have to stop him before *they* get him too."

"I don't think it's working," said Kristy.

"Should we go after him?" he asked.

"And then what?" asked Kristy.

Mateo hated feeling so helpless, but Carl had forged his own fate. Like a renegade, not like a team player. *Carl is putting us all at risk!* Mateo's thoughts shouted. *How does he think he can just walk into the valley, into the middle of eight killer spirits, and save Priya? Is he planning on asking them nicely? Pretty please and thank you, with sugar on top?* It seemed like a suicide mission.

Carl stumbled on some loose rocks as the hill became steeper. He barely maintained his footing, but the spirits ignored his clumsy approach.

"He's going to fall," said Kristy. "He's moving too fast."

"Any idea what he's going to do once he gets down there?" asked Mateo.

Kristy shrugged. "No clue."

"I hope he has some kind of plan," said Mateo.

"Don't count on it," she said.

Carl stumbled again, and this time he fell. Hard. Kristy and Mateo gasped as Carl screamed and rolled down the loose gravel hill, turning a couple of rough somersaults before landing in a heap at the bottom of an embankment. "Augh!" he screamed again and reached for his ankle.

"I knew it," said Kristy. She turned to Mateo. "Now what?"

"We help him." Mateo walked back toward the edge of the cliff. "What else?"

"Hold on!" Kristy ran up to him. "Look!"

Mateo stopped and looked into the valley. The spirits were frozen, no longer oblivious to the intruder in their midst. They must have heard Carl, and now each and every one of them was looking in his direction.

"Carl!" Mateo yelled. "Get out of there!"

"Carl!" screamed Kristy.

Carl didn't need their warnings. He had already seen the spirits—and now they were moving straight toward him.

"I can't watch!" said Kristy.

"Get down," said Mateo. They both went to the ground, lying on their stomachs. No need to risk being seen themselves. They kept their eyes on Carl. "I feel like we should do something."

"What can we do?" said Kristy.

The eight spirits darted over to Carl. He scratched and clawed his way a few feet up the cliff, but with his injured ankle, it was no use. "Mateo! Help!"

"This is horrible," said Mateo. "I need to help him." He tried getting up, but Kristy pulled him back down.

"You go down there and the same thing that happened to Priya, the same thing that's about to happen to Carl, will happen to you," she said. "You're smarter than that."

"But how can you just—" Another noise interrupted Mateo's question, the same awful moaning they had heard when the spirit entered Priya's body. A white spirit hovered above Carl, now lying slack on the ground, and then morphed into a long plume of smoke and buried itself in Carl's body.

CHAPTER 10

"How could we let that happen?" asked Mateo as Carl's body floated with an escort of spirits toward Priya's resting place. His body settled into the tall grass next to hers. The spirits resumed their dance.

"What were we supposed to do?" asked Kristy. "Carl made it next to impossible for us to help him. If you had run down there to save him, you probably would've tripped too. And now you'd be lying in the grass with the two of them and I'd be up here all by myself." She grabbed his shoulder. "Carl made a mistake. We can't do the same thing. We can't afford to. Our friends' lives are in our hands, and what we need to do now is put all our energy into thinking of a way to save Priya and Carl."

Mateo nodded. "You're right." He looked at her and shook his head, feeling overwhelmed. "But what the heck can we do? Look at the moon. It's almost time."

Kristy looked and nodded. "You're right. But we're going to think of something. We have to. They're depending on us."

"Okay, then," said Mateo. "Let's think."

They sat in silence for a minute.

"Well," said Kristy. "It's too late to find help."

"For sure," said Mateo. "And we don't have a way to call anybody."

"That's right," said Kristy.

"So it's definitely up to us," said Mateo. The sky was getting darker. Stars twinkled above them.

"What about this?" said Mateo. "We create a fire. We start it in just the right place so that the smoke rises up and blocks the moonlight from hitting their faces."

"You have a match?" asked Kristy.

"Nope." Mateo shook his head.

"You know how to start a fire without one?"

"Nope," said Mateo.

They sat in the quiet some more.

"I've got it," said Kristy. "We wait up here for the blood moon. A few minutes before it happens we go down into that valley—more cautiously than Carl—and we snatch their bodies. We pull them under the shade of the trees and prevent the moonlight from hitting their faces."

Mateo scratched his head.

"I know," she said. "Stupid idea. The spirits will see us before we have a chance to get to them, and they'll just turn us into zombies when they do."

Mateo looked away. He thought back to Carl, crashing down the hill, screaming in pain, and what the spirits had done right after that. "Wait a second," he said. "Wait a second. Your plan's not half-bad."

"What?"

"You said the spirits will see us," said Mateo. "But the spirits didn't *see* Carl. Not until he fell and screamed, right?"

"Right," said Kristy.

"They heard him fall, then they saw him," said Mateo. "It was his scream that alerted them, then they went to him. And how many of them did that?"

"All of them," she said. "What's your point?"

"When the spirits saw Carl—" said Mateo.

"They *all* left." Kristy interrupted. She got it. "They all left their spot in the meadow. They all flew over to Carl. Not one of them stayed behind with Priya."

"That's right," said Mateo. "So your plan is a pretty good one."

"It is?" she asked.

"With just a couple adjustments," said Mateo. He put his hands on Kristy's shoulders and looked her square in the eye. "Let me explain."

CHAPTER 11

Mateo waited on the ridge, his back to a boulder and his knees tucked up to his chest. By now Kristy had hopefully crawled down the side of the canyon and hidden herself among the trees at the edge of the meadow.

That next step would have to wait just a little longer. The timing had to be perfect or the whole thing would crash and burn.

Mateo looked at the stars. They reminded him of his dad. On clear nights like this, when Mateo was younger, his dad would take him into the country. They'd find a place in the middle of nowhere, far away from the city lights, and watch the shimmering stars for hours. Neither of them had ever learned the names of any of the constellations or the locations of the planets, but they both loved the night. His dad said stargazing was one of the only fond memories he had of his years working the fields up and down the California valleys. After working a twelve- or fourteen-hour day, he and Mateo's mom would hold each other under the big California sky, dream of better days, and forget for a few minutes that tomorrow would bring another shift of backbreaking day labor.

My parents have given their lives for me, Mateo thought. *Every choice they've made has been about helping me have a better life, a different life from theirs. Why has it taken me so long to finally figure that out?* Mateo thought back to the arguments he'd had with his dad over the years, arguments about dumb things like drinking milk directly from the carton or how he would refuse to take his ball cap off when they ate at nice restaurants. How he'd get annoyed when his mom wanted him to help her put the groceries away or take out the trash. *I've been so stupid, so disrespectful. It's*

*time I grow up and show my parents how much
I appreciate what they're doing to help me. When
they were my age they were sneaking across the
California border, unsure if they'd make it into
this country alive, uncertain where they'd find
their next meal or where they'd sleep for the night.
I spend my days angry if there aren't enough chips
in the house. If I disappear tonight, what will they
think? They'll remember me starting arguments
over dumb things.*

But I can fix it now, he thought. *If I get out
of this alive, I can tell Mom and Dad how much
they mean to me and how proud I am to be their
son. They deserve better than how I've treated them
these past few years.*

He suddenly pictured his parents as
teenagers, crossing the US border with their
families, cowering together under the cover of
darkness. His mom had told him stories about
seeing guards in the distance with automatic
weapons strapped to their bodies. She had held
her breath for minutes at a time, worried that
the sound of her breathing would give them
away. *Mom and Dad are the most courageous*

people I know. If they had the guts to make the dangerous journey to America, I can certainly do what's necessary to save my friends.

Mateo turned and looked behind him. The moon was barely more than a sliver. Below him the spirits, the jet-black ones, the brilliant-white ones, and the steel-gray ones, still wove their bizarre circle above Carl and Priya. The more he watched their beguiling dance, the more the spirits seemed as normal as the trees or the tall grass or the rocky slope around them.

Their plan had to work. It had to. If it didn't, then what? Carl and Priya would be gone forever, and he and Kristy would have to explain what had happened to them. If they mentioned ghost trucks and dancing spirits and abductions, they'd both end up in some funny farm. If they didn't mention those things, people would have no choice but to think they murdered Carl and Priya. It would be just like the girl from Sleepy Cove who went missing. Her friends weren't thrown into jail for murder, but maybe he and Kristy would be.

Maybe the trial would mean Cal Poly wouldn't let him in. Maybe they'd get convicted and go to prison for a very long time. Who knows? Maybe they'd be locked up forever.

He shook his head. *Stop thinking that way,* he said to himself. *First of all, you're going to save Priya and Carl. Second of all, if for some reason your plan fails and the worst happens, you should be thinking about your friends and not yourself. They are the ones who will have the truly horrific future.*

Mateo shivered and hugged himself in the cold. He had given his jacket to Kristy. All part of the plan. He hoped she was going to be okay. He didn't worry about her navigating her way down the rock face. She was a natural-born climber. He was sure she was at the bottom by now. But he worried about whether she'd stay safe during what was about to happen next.

Kristy really stepped up, thought Mateo. *She was so scared earlier, scared enough that I thought she'd just lost it.* But ever since they had fixed their minds on rescuing Priya, ever since their backs had been thrown hard up against the wall, she had stepped up. When Mateo told her his plan involved them splitting up and her going into the valley to face the spirits by herself, at least at first, he wondered if that would be too much for her. But it wasn't. She was down with it, ready to do this crazy thing Mateo thought might work. Kristy's strength and courage during this wild, eerie night surpassed his own. The two of them had agreed on their final actions, hugged, and somewhat reluctantly said their good-byes.

Mateo looked into the sky behind him once again. The blood moon was just minutes away. If he acted too early, Kristy might not be ready and the plan could be a complete bust. If he waited too long, the crimson glow would shine on the faces of his friends and it would all be over. His timing had to be just right.

He stared at the moon. He could see the last bit of yellow disappearing before his eyes. Smaller and smaller the moon shrank away. The night was growing darker. *You need to wait*, he told himself. *Wait. Just a few more seconds.* His heart was pumping. Clouds of white steam burst from his mouth in an even rhythm. *Wait.*

*Wait. A little bit longer. Just like a race. Wait for
that starting gun to go off. Take off too soon and
you'll be disqualified. Wait too long and you'll be
behind the pack.*

One last look. *Okay. This is it. Ten seconds.
Five.* Mateo closed his eyes, took two last deep
breaths. "Here we go," he said to himself.
"Kristy, I hope you're ready."

Mateo jumped to his feet. "Hey, you
freaks!" he shouted into the valley. It was the
shout of his life, the loudest one he had ever
made. "Up here! Up here, you freaks! Leave
my friends alone and come and get me! Let's
see how tough you are now. Come on, freaks!
Come and get me!"

The spirits turned toward him. He could
feel the power of their combined stare as a
gust of wind blew through him. He whispered,
"That's it, you weirdos. That's it. Now come
and get me."

"Up here!" he shouted and waved his arms
in the air. "What are you waiting for? Come
and get me!" He lobbed some rocks at them for
good measure.

Suddenly, the spirits were on the move, heading straight toward him. "Crap," he said. "It's working. Okay, here we go."

He took one last look into the valley. He couldn't be sure, but he thought he saw a dark shape sprint from the trees and toward the torches. He hoped with every last hope that it was Kristy.

Mateo took off running, away from the valley. He darted around trees and up and over rocks. His strides were long. He channeled the cross-country speedster still inside him and thought back to his countless races through pristine, green golf courses and along rugged, wooded paths. He let out a short laugh. *There's a difference, though. A big difference. Instead of being followed by competitors from other teams who want to take the first-place medal from me, I'm being pursued by creatures who want to steal my soul.* He couldn't help but see a little humor in it.

Mateo ran. He ran hard and fast. He felt alive, relaxed, his legs pushing his body forward, his arms pumping, his lungs expanding to suck in every last ounce of life-giving air. Running had always worked to calm him down. *Why in the world did I ever quit?* he wondered. *Was it really because I wanted more time to work on the jeep, or did it have more to do with Dad? Was it just some ridiculous act of rebellion to show Dad I'm a grown-up who can make his own decisions? Is that possible?* He thought so. That was it. *Wow, what an idiot.* He had stopped running because he knew it would have an effect on his dad. *I'm such a jerk.*

He made another quick deal with himself. *Survive this night and you're rejoining the team. End of story.*

His thoughts flashed back to the business at hand. He let out another loud shout. "This way, you animals!" He had to make sure he didn't lose the spirits in the trees. They needed to follow him deep into the woods and far away from his friends. "Come and get me, freaks!"

He glanced over his shoulder. No need to worry about losing them. The spirits were right there. *Man, they're quick.* He wished he could stop and count them, to make sure each and every spirit was there and that none had stayed behind with Priya and Carl. The success of their plan rested on that extremely crucial detail.

The air around him suddenly became frigid, like he had been magically transported to an ice sheet at the South Pole. His fingers and toes froze up. An instant later he glimpsed movement out of the corner of his eye. The spirits had caught up to him. His run was over. Two black spirits floated down in front of him to cut off his path. Mateo stopped. Up close, they were big—bigger than he'd realized. From the bottom of their robes to the top of their hoods, the spirits were eight feet tall at least. Mateo turned. Two grayish spirits were directly behind him. The rest closed in on him from the other directions. He did a quick count. Seven. That was all of them.

Slowly and gracefully, a bright white spirit floated up and over him. Mateo looked into its eyes. They were dark sockets, deep voids sunk into the shadows of the smoky skull. The face was mesmerizing. In a way, beautiful.

Mateo couldn't take his eyes off it. It drifted and floated in the breeze, constantly shifting shapes. Mateo felt a warmth go through him, a calmness, a happiness. All his worries seemed to wash away. His body felt light. Nothing mattered. He forgot where he was and why. He was completely at peace.

But something pulled him back. The white spirit began to take on a reddish glow. It broke from Mateo's gaze and turned its face to the moon.

Mateo snapped from his trance. Everything came rushing back. "The blood moon," he said out loud. "It must be starting."

The white spirit let out its mind-shattering shriek. Mateo dropped to his knees and protected his ears from the noise as the rest of the spirits joined in. The sound was haunting. Deafening. Awful. He looked up to see the clustered spirits staring at the moon. They seemed distressed, as if they knew something was terribly wrong. Mateo remembered to keep his own face out of the moonlight. "Don't look at it," he muttered to himself. "Don't look."

All at once the spirits scattered. They turned their backs to the moon and quickly fled toward the valley.

Kristy!

Mateo jumped to his feet and ran after them.

CHAPTER 12

Mateo ran like never before in his life. The spirits were ahead of him, flying above the trees. Soon they would dip out of view into the valley. He ran like the wind, like a thoroughbred horse, like a hungry cheetah in pursuit of dinner. He didn't stop to think what might happen if he tripped on a root or a rock in his path. He just ran. Kristy's life, and the lives of Carl and Priya, depended on him. He needed to get to them in time.

He made it to the edge of the embankment, skidding to a stop at the spot where the terrain took a severe downward trajectory. A cloud of dust rose around his feet. Below Mateo the spirits were descending upon his friends. His earlier plan had been to take a safer route into the valley, the path Kristy had used, avoiding the steepest sections of cliff. He had thought he might be able to keep the spirits away from Kristy, Priya, and Carl until the full blood moon was complete. But that clearly hadn't happened. As the spirits raced toward his friends, Mateo made a snap judgment. He needed to get to Kristy fast, to help her, as quickly as possible. He chose Carl's path.

Stay on your feet, just stay on your feet, he told himself. But he built up far too much speed on the first yards of the incline, and he went down. He bounced and tumbled, then came to a stop. He did a quick body check. *No broken bones. Let's go.* Before him was the patch of loose rocks and the drop that had gotten the better of Carl. Mateo made a quick calculation in his mind: *jump.* It might be a steep drop, but he didn't think the section of cliff could be higher than about ten feet. He could make it. He kept up his speed and at the last possible second dug his left foot into the dirt and sailed through the air.

The jump seemed like more than ten feet. As he began to think he'd maybe made a mistake and completely blown up the plan, he hit the ground and rolled, out of control, three or four or five times. Gravel scratched at his hands and his elbows. Winded, he checked himself again, already moving toward his friends. The damage was minimal. There would be bruises and scrapes to deal with later, but his knees and ankles and legs were fine. Time to run.

He entered the valley—luckily flat for the most part—and was just a hundred feet or so from his friends. "Hold on, Kristy!" he shouted. "I'm coming!"

Mateo remembered the calm feelings he had experienced while looking into the face of the white spirit—a trance! "Don't look at them!" he yelled. "Kristy, whatever you do, don't look them in the face!" He ran. He was almost there. He could see Kristy kneeling over Carl and Priya, covering their faces with her jacket and the one Mateo had given her. The spirits surrounded her, moaning some wretched sound he hadn't heard them make before.

"Don't look them in the eye!" Mateo made it. He finally made it. He dove through the torches and crashed on top of his friends.

"Help me!" screamed Kristy. "I can't hang on!"

Mateo saw it. Kristy's body was being pulled into the air by some unseen force. She was barely keeping her hands on the jackets that covered Priya and Carl's faces. Mateo grabbed hold of his jacket, the one that was covering Carl, and at the same time snagged Kristy's leg with his other hand to keep her from floating away. "Hang on!" he yelled. "It's almost over!" *Priya said this would be a short eclipse*, he thought. *Only two minutes. Two minutes.* How long ago was it that the spirits, hovering over him, shrieked at the blood moon and scurried back to the valley? It had to have been a minute at least. This nightmare would be over soon.

"Hang on, Kristy!" he shouted again. He held his jacket over Carl's face. The moaning grew louder. Gusts of wind battered his body; the temperature had dropped significantly. His fingers were beginning to freeze and stiffen up.

Then he felt his own body begin to rise. He and Kristy were both being pulled away from their friends. "Keep the jackets over their faces!" he shouted. "Don't let go!"

"I won't if you don't!" yelled Kristy.

It was all Mateo could do to keep his body on the ground, his face turned away, his hands on the jacket. "Come on, you stupid blood moon!" he screamed. "Be done, for crying out loud. Let's end this thing!"

As if someone was following his orders, Mateo's body suddenly dropped to the ground. Kristy's did the same. They scrambled to get a better grip on the jackets, to protect their friends. "What's going on?" Kristy yelled.

"I'm not sure!" Mateo said. "But don't look up!" Maybe the full blood moon had ended, but he didn't want to relax just yet.

The spirits' moans quickly turned to terrible wails that pierced Mateo's eardrums. He grimaced. It was the most pain he'd ever experienced in his life, but he refused to let go of the jacket to protect his ears. He tried to ride it out.

"They're leaving!" yelled Kristy.

"I told you not to look!" screamed Mateo.

His eyes were still on the ground, but when he realized that the awful shrieks from the spirits were getting quieter, he couldn't help but do the same. He looked up into the sky.

The spirits were now at least fifty feet above them, turning in a compact circle, wailing and flying up higher and higher into the night. Their flight became faster. Their circle became tighter.

"Look out!" shouted Kristy.

Mateo looked over to her. She had pulled back, leaving the jacket over Priya's face but inching away from her body. Coming out from Priya's nose and open mouth was the same white spirit they had seen enter her earlier in the night. Mateo looked at Carl. The other spirit was leaving his body. Mateo slowly retreated.

The two spirits coalesced again, robes billowing in the icy wind, and flew into the sky to join the others. Together the spirits morphed into one large cloud of smoke, shot up into the air, and were gone. Just like that, it was over.

CHAPTER 13

"Where am I?" Priya was sitting up in the grass. "What happened?" She rubbed her head. Carl was propped up on his elbows. Kristy and Mateo were seated next to them.

"You're safe now." Kristy massaged her back. "It's all over."

"What's over?" asked Priya.

"Don't you remember?" asked Mateo.

Looking confused, Priya ruffled her fingers through her hair. "Wait a minute," she said. "The blood moon. We were going to watch the blood moon. Did I miss it?"

"You did," said Mateo. He and Kristy shared a laugh.

"What's so funny?" asked Priya.

"You really don't remember anything?" asked Kristy. "The spirits? Us running through the woods? The truck?"

"The truck!" she shouted. "Yeah, I remember. There was an old hunk of junk pickup trying to run us off the road. I remember that." She stopped. "Wait a minute. Did you say something about spirits?"

Carl was holding his ankle. "She did," he said. "There was a smoke spirit with a skeleton face. It entered your body and took you off into the woods. Hey, how did I hurt my leg?"

"A spirit took me into the woods?" asked Priya. "Are you serious? And I don't remember anything? That really stinks, man."

Mateo laughed. "Unbelievable."

Kristy punched Priya's shoulder, knocking her back a bit. "We saved your life, girl," said Kristy. "How about showing some gratitude?"

"You should've seen our man over here try to rescue you," joked Mateo. "Carl went tumbling down that hill and got himself abducted too."

"I did?" asked Carl. "Cool."

Kristy could only shake her head. "Can we get out of here?" she asked. "Before those things decide to come back?"

"I second that idea," said Mateo.

They got up. Priya and Carl wobbled on weak legs. "Steady now," said Kristy as she held onto Priya. Carl stood on his one good foot and leaned on Mateo's shoulder.

"It could be morning before we get your sorry butts back home," said Mateo. He helped Carl forward. "Let's go hop along."

The group limped toward the edge of the valley, toward the ridge and away from the most bizarre scene of their lives.

"Hey," said Carl. "I just thought of something ironic. We wanted a night to remember, right?"

"Right," said Kristy.

"Ha," said Carl. "Well, Priya can't remember any of it!"

Mateo and Kristy laughed. "Good one, funny man," said Priya. "I remember that you have no future in stand-up comedy."

"It's a night I won't ever forget," said Kristy. "How about you, Mateo?"

"Not likely," he said.

"You have to tell me everything," said Priya as they neared the hill. "All the gory details."

"That shouldn't be a problem," said Mateo. "We've got all night, and we'll need something to pass the time. Kristy, you want to do the honors?"

"Sure," she said.

"No," interrupted Carl. "Let me."

Kristy chuckled. "The floor is all yours."

"Okay," he said. "It's like this. We were driving up the PCH in Mateo's boss yellow jeep. The moon was full and bright over the Pacific, and a fog was just starting to dissolve in the saltwater air. The music was cranking, the girls were dancing, and life was good. Then, suddenly, out of nowhere, from the darkness, appears a phantom tan pickup truck."

Mateo and Kristy shared a smile. The walk back to the jeep was going to take a while. Carl's recap of their night, though, would likely take even longer.

Mateo was really looking forward to getting back into the jeep, onto the PCH, and back to the comfort of his home. Tomorrow he would have a good long run and a good long talk with his parents. He could hardly wait.

ABOUT THE AUTHOR

Chris Kreie is an elementary school teacher and lives in Minnesota with his wife and two children. As a kid, he always loved scary stories. Now he enjoys biking, traveling, hiking, and spending time at his family's cabin—especially during a full moon.